# Don't Touch

Written by Josephine Selwyn

# Picture Dictionary

cactus

fire

knife

Read the picture dictionary. You will find these words in the book.

liquid

medicine

stove top

Don't touch that stove top. It is hot.

pot

Don't touch that knife.
It is sharp.

edge

Don't touch that cactus.
It is prickly.

needle

Don't touch that fire.
It is burning.

Don't touch that liquid.
It is poisonous.

bottle

Don't touch that medicine. It is dangerous.

nasal spray

multi-symptom
**daytime**
cold/flu relief
non-drowsy/alcohol free/antihistamine free
nasal decongestant / pain reliever
cough suppressant / fever reducer
**6 FL OZ (177 mL)**

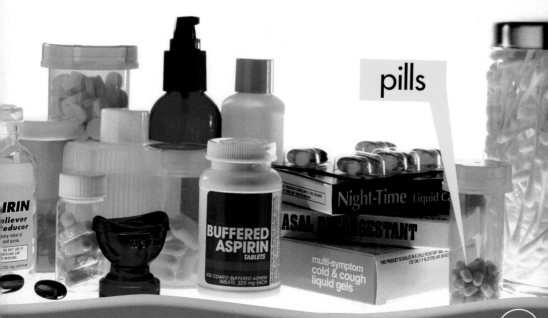

pills

IRIN
eliever
educer

BUFFERED
ASPIRIN
*TABLETS*

Night-Time Liquid Ca

ASAL DECONGESTANT

multi-symptom
cold & cough
liquid gels

# Activity Page

1. Draw one of the things in the book.

2. Copy this caption:
   Don't touch that. It is _____.

Do you know the dictionary words?